D1227658

To Declan and Archer — my two shining stars. And to Chad, my partner on this journey. Special thanks to Cathy Cruise, Meg Moody, Art Taylor, Ruby Chase, and the countless others who offered feedback and encouragement. I appreciate all of you so much. Mom, Dad, and Sarah — thanks for giving me the courage to reach for the stars.
— L.C.B.

For Corrie, Noah, and Lily. You are my inspiration and joy. Thanks for putting up with me.
— J.H.

Copyright © 2020 Lindsay C. Barry
Illustrations copyright © 2020 Benjamin Hoyle

All rights reserved. No part of this publication may be reproduced, stored in a retrieval system, or transmitted, in any form or by any means, electronic, mechanical, photocopying, recording, or otherwise, without the prior written permission of the author.

This book is a work of fiction. Any references to historical events, real people, or real places are used fictitiously. Other names, characters, places, and events are products of the author's imagination, and any resemblance to actual events or places or persons, living or dead, is entirely coincidental.

Library of Congress Cataloging-in-Publication Data
Names: Barry, Lindsay C., author. | Hoyle, Jamin, illustrator.
Title: Journey to Constellation Station / by Lindsay C. Barry ; illustrated by Jamin Hoyle.
Description: Santa Fe, NM : Santa Fe Writers Project, [2020] | Audience: Ages 5-10. | Audience: Grades K-1. | Summary: Illustrations and rhyming text invite the reader on an interstellar train ride to Constellation Station, where they will learn about the galaxy and constellations.
Identifiers: LCCN 2019048053 (print) | LCCN 2019048054 (ebook) | ISBN 9781733777797 (pbk.) | ISBN 9781951631000 (ebook)
Subjects: CYAC: Stories in rhyme. | Constellations—Fiction. | Milky Way—Fiction.
Classification: LCC PZ8.3.B253652 Jou 2020 (print) | LCC PZ8.3.B253652 (ebook) | DDC [E]—dc23
LC record available at https://lccn.loc.gov/2019048053
LC ebook record available at https://lccn.loc.gov/2019048054

Published by City Different Books,
an imprint of the Santa Fe Writers Project
369 Montezuma Ave. #350
Santa Fe, NM 87501
(505) 428-9045
sfwp.com

City Different Books

Find the author at: lbarrybooks.com

Marysville Public Library
231 S. Plum Street
Marysville, OH 43040
937-642-1876

DISCARD

JOURNEY TO CONSTELLATION STATION

By Lindsay C. Barry

Illustrated by Jamin Hoyle

Do you have your ticket?
ALL YOU DO
is close your eyes.

The rails are ready to take you on a
STARRY NIGHT SURPRISE.

Climb up on the train and bring your stellar imagination.

All aboard! It's time to depart for

CONSTELLATION STATION.

Constellation Station
is in our galaxy,

THE MILKY WAY.

While the journey there is lightning fast,
all you'll feel is the gentle sway

of train cars with windows wide,
open to the starry night.

Look out and see man-made space art —

A TWIRLING SATELLITE!

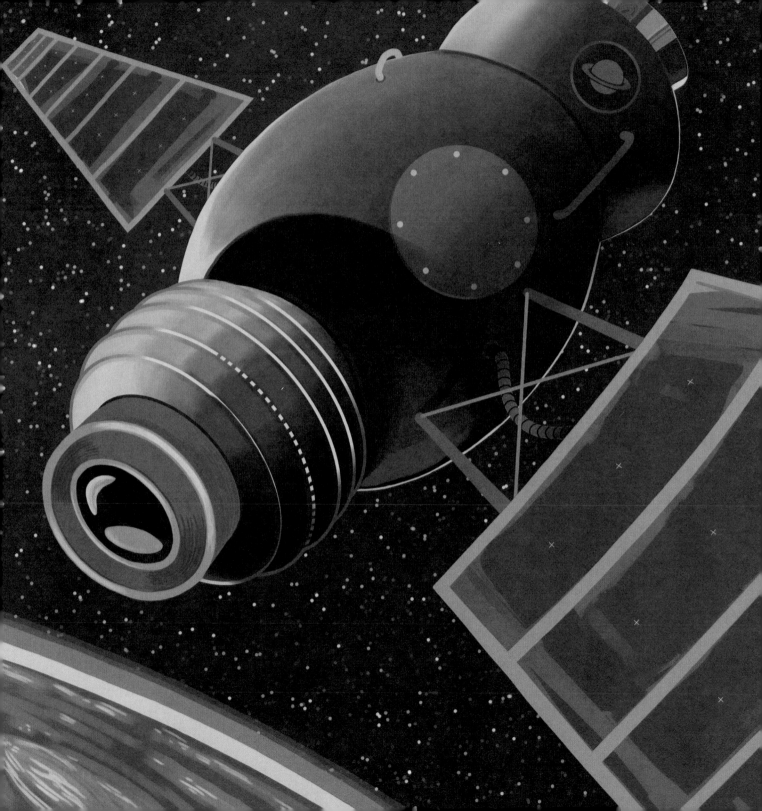

CHUGGING PAST THE MOON,
reflecting the sun's brilliant glow,

stars pulse and shine and blink,
all above, around, and below.

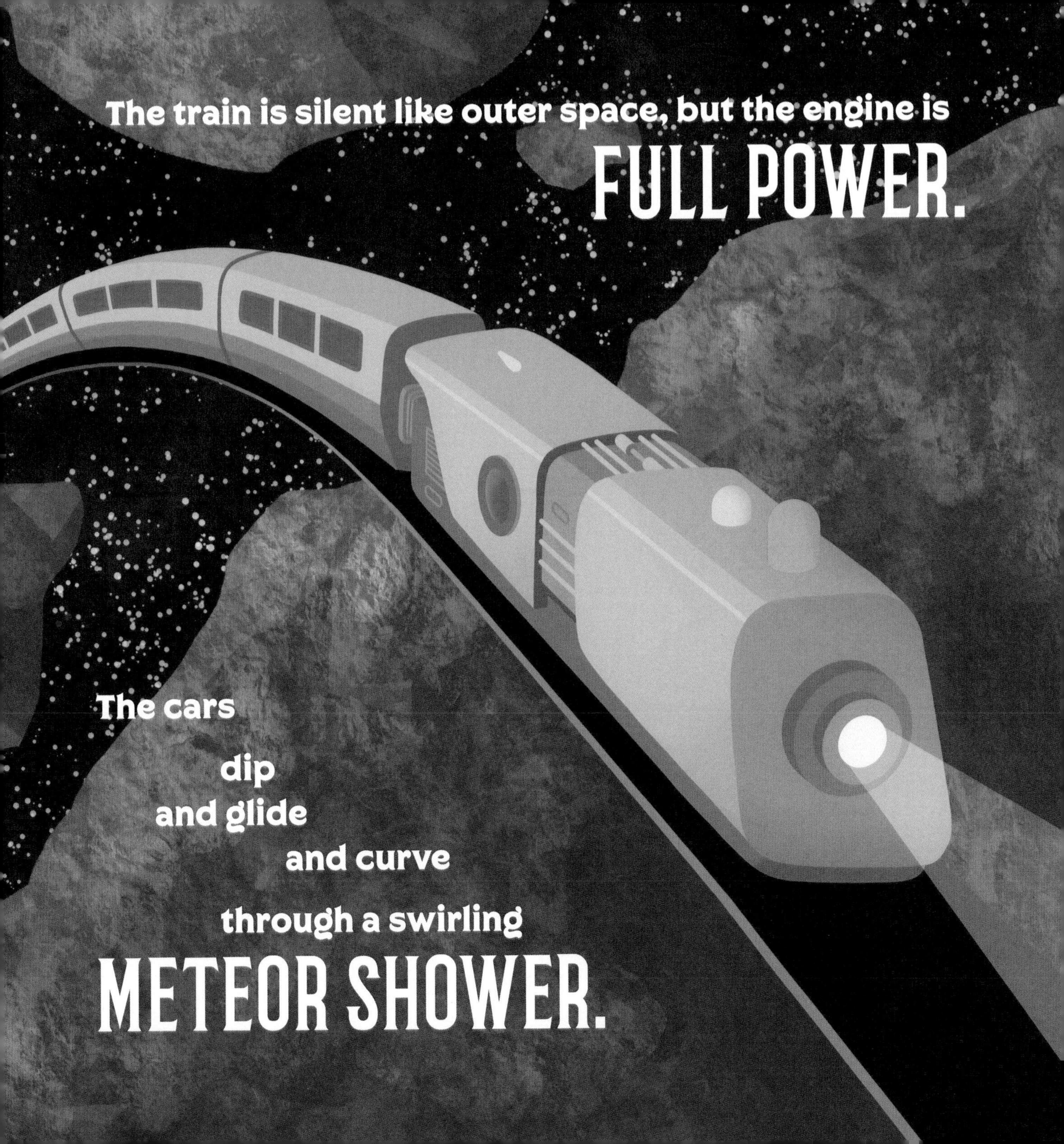

The train is silent like outer space, but the engine is

FULL POWER.

The cars

dip

and glide

and curve

through a swirling

METEOR SHOWER.

Puff through a

BLACK HOLE TUNNEL,
speed along the terrestrial track.

Come out and view the

COLORS OF SPACE,
brilliant against the black.

THERE IT IS!

The platform swirls in starry-bright rotation.

Punch your ticket and disembark.

YOU'VE REACHED CONSTELLATION STATION!

Not many have come before you — it's a

SPECIAL PART OF SPACE.

And if you look for it on a map, it will vanish

WITHOUT A TRACE.

In the station's silent center is a

TELESCOPE OF STARS.

Each point shows a

CONSTELLATION,

no matter how faint or far.

Leo the Lion
ROARS INTO VIEW,
his mane his crowning jewel.

Pick another point
and
focus your eye on

TAURUS
the
charging bull.

Scorpius the Scorpion strikes and stings,
his tail towering high.

Now see graceful Cygnus the Swan,
wings stretched across the sky.

The Great Dog howls across the black,
signaling his slumber,

While the Great Bear shakes the stars awake
with his heavy-footed lumber.

Another star points to Gemini,
twin brothers
SHINING DOUBLE.

Pisces the Fish shows a night-swimming pair, each breath

A GLOWING BUBBLE.

The winged-horse
PEGASUS
sparkles mid-air, rearing up
FOR FLIGHT.

Orion
THE HUNTER
poses with sword, shield raised
READY TO FIGHT.

Libra the Scales keeps sky in balance,
WEIGHING CELESTIAL LAWS.

Cancer the Crab side-steps the stars,
GRASPING WITH HIS CLAWS.

Now it's time to journey home,

THE CARS ARE GLIDING PAST.

Board the train for a last view

OF THE GALAXY SO VAST.

Visit nightly to view
THE STARS
at their highest elevation.

Just close your eyes, and come back again, to

CONSTELLATION STATION.

Why Read *Journey to Constellation Station*?

Thank you for reading *Journey to Constellation Station*, which I hope was an exciting foray into outer space for you and your children. *Journey to Constellation Station* is a vehicle that can open a conversation as to how we, as humans, are all connected, and a tool that parents, teachers and caregivers can use to discuss the night sky, science, and the power of the imagination.

We all live under the same sky, and though we have different backgrounds and beliefs, the beautiful tapestry of stars above us has always told a story in our collective folklores and traditions. Rocket launches, solar eclipses, and other major events in space bring the world together. Throughout history, famous figures and ordinary people alike have all looked upwards at the stars, naming them and crafting stories around them — and we still use those names and tell those stories today. For children and adults alike, this mutual fascination has persisted throughout human history. Who hasn't looked up at the night sky and been awed? And while our own world changes almost daily, many of the stars you can show your children have burned brightly and unchanged for countless eons.

We are still searching the sky, dreaming and exploring. It's ingrained in us as humans, and this fascination starts at a young age. We learn about the galaxy and solar system, great moments in space history, the names of the planets, and the names of the people who have brought us to those places.

Reading *Journey to Constellation Station* with a child will help open up the amazing world of the night sky and outer space, help us teach our children about the history of the stars, and encourage the understanding that the night sky is something everyone in the world shares.

Journey to Constellation Station also addresses sleep issues, and can be used to help your children get restful sleep and explore their imaginations. But don't let that stop you from making time to journey out with a child as the stars are appearing to see who can spot the first one, or plan a weekend night where it's a treat to stay up a little later and see what constellations you can view.

Journey to Constellation Station touches on constellations of course, but also various other

space-related terms like galaxies, the Milky Way, black holes, etc. Kids will be excited to take a closer look at the night sky and discover what constellations they can see. I have included a glossary of some common terms related to our night sky, and that are mentioned in this book. You can find it on the next few pages.

The STEM Connection

Journey to Constellation Station is creative and artistic, but also emphasizes Science, Technology, Engineering and Math (STEM) and is a great resource when teaching units on space.

On my webpage, lbarrybooks.com, I have developed a few STEM activities that go along with the book and are free to access. I am always eager to see your own artwork and projects related to the book, and I have also created a gallery of reader-submitted projects that may provide additional ideas for teaching your children about the night sky! Please feel free to submit your own projects via the contact form on my website, and you can find me on Instagram and Twitter @lbarrybooks.

The Constellations

Many of the constellations featured in *Journey to Constellation Station* are also in the Zodiac. In astronomy, the Zodiac is closely tied to how the Earth moves through the sky. In astrology, the Zodiac is made of 12 signs that reflect the position of the sun when you were born. Some people believe that this has a strong influence on your personality, character, and emotions. The Ancient Greeks first determined the 12 star signs and much of Greek mythology is related to the stars and constellations.

Help your children spot these constellations in the night sky so they, too, can find Leo the Lion, Scorpius the Scorpion, Pegasus, and others.

For a guide to the stars and stargazing, check out the free online planetarium at in-the-sky.org.

Three Additional Activities to Try with Your Kids

1. Pretend you are in outer space. What do you think it's like there? Hot or cold? Loud or quiet?

2. "Camp" outside (this can be as easy as a blanket, flashlight and *Journey to Constellation Station*). What sounds do you hear at night outside? What do you think people in different countries or states hear and see?

3. Lay on a blanket and let your eyes adjust to the darkness. What do you see above you? Stars? Anything else? What's the brightest item you can see in the sky?

Space Facts to Share with Your Kids

Space is completely silent. It would be a good place to get some reading done! There are 200-400 billion stars in our galaxy alone. That's a lot of wishes! 1.3 million Earths could fit inside the Sun.

The first astronauts to walk on the moon were Neil Armstrong and Buzz Aldrin (in that order). They made the first moon walk on July 20, 1969. Since then, 10 additional astronauts have walked on the moon (12 total).

The rise and fall of the tides on Earth is caused by the Moon.

Train Facts to Share with Your Kids

There are three types of trains: electric, diesel and steam.

The first steam train was built in 1804. Ask your children to figure out how long ago that was. Can they imagine what the world was like for the people seeing the steam engine for the first time?

The world's fastest train is the Shanghai Maglev in China. This train travels about 19 miles from an airport and takes about seven minutes for its journey, traveling at top speeds of 267 mph!

The world's longest passenger train is The Ghan in Australia. This train pulls an average of 26 carriages and covers a distance of 1,851 miles in about 54 hours.

Journey to Constellation Station Glossary

Learning isn't over after the last page is read! The glossary below defines some of the bigger words used throughout this book. Parents and caregivers — go back through with your kids and ask them if they know what these words mean. If not, read them the definitions and discuss!

BLACK HOLE: A black hole is a place in space where gravity is so strong, even light cannot get out. We can't actually see black holes...they are invisible! Space telescopes with special tools can help us find them.

CELESTIAL: Celestial means something that has to do with the sky, or outer space.

CONSTELLATION: A constellation is a group of stars that forms a recognizable pattern. Our ancestors named these patterns after animals or figures from their myths and legends. There are currently 88 named constellations.

The first great astronomer was named Ptolemy, who identified 48 constellations. It wasn't until more than 1,500 years later when sailors named the remaining 40.

GALAXY: A galaxy is a large group of stars. We don't know how many galaxies are out there — it could be billions, or even trillions!

METEOR SHOWER: A meteor is a space rock that enters Earth's atmosphere. As the space rock falls toward Earth, it gets really hot and glows, causing us see a "shooting star."

When Earth encounters many meteors at once, we call it a meteor shower. Meteor showers are named after the constellation where the meteors appear to be coming from. For example, the Orionids Meteor Shower, which occurs in October each year, appear to be originating near the constellation Orion the Hunter.

SATELLITE: A satellite is an object in space that circles around a bigger object. There are two kinds of satellites: natural (like the moon) or artificial (like the International Space Station). In *Journey to Constellation Station* I call satellites man-made space art!

Artificial satellites are launched into space to do a specific job. Weather stations might launch a satellite to help predict the weather. Your favorite shows are beamed to outer space and back!

STELLAR: The first definition of stellar is that it describes anything that relates to the stars. But there is a second meaning. In *Journey to Constellation Station*, I encourage you to use your "stellar imagination." In that case, stellar can mean "outstanding," or "of high quality." If you get an A+ on a test, that is a stellar grade!

TERRESTRIAL: Terrestrial means something that has to do with the Earth. In *Journey to Constellation Station* I say, "speed along the terrestrial track." The track is starting from Earth and reaching out into outer space. If something is extraterrestrial, it's outside the earth.

THE MILKY WAY: The Earth is located in the spiral-shaped galaxy called The Milky Way. It's called The Milky Way because of its milky appearance from Earth, which is caused by far-away stars.

NAMES AND FUN FACTS

CANCER: The constellation Cancer is located in the northern sky. Its name means "the crab" in Latin. Cancer is the hardest to see of the 12 zodiac constellations.

For Parents: There are two versions in Greek mythology associated with Cancer as a crab. One is that Hera sends a crab to distract Hercules while the hero is fighting Hydra, the serpent-like beast with many heads and poisonous breath. When the crab tries to harm Hercules, Hercules kicks it all the way to the stars.

In another version, the crab gets crushed instead and Hera, a sworn enemy of Hercules, places it in the sky for its efforts. However, because the crab was not successful in hurting Hercules, Hera places the crab in a region of the sky that has no bright stars.

CASTOR AND POLLUX: Castor and Pollux were twin half-brothers in Greek and Roman mythology. Castor was mortal and Pollux was immortal. Pollux asked Zeus to let him share his own immortality with his twin to keep them together, and they were transformed into the constellation Gemini.

CYGNUS: "Cygnus" is Latin for "swan" and is associated with the Greek myth of Zeus and Leda. Cygnus was first catalogued by the Greek astronomer Ptolemy. Cygnus is a northern constellation lying on the plane of the Milky Way and is the 16th largest constellation in the night sky.

GEMINI: Gemini is Latin for "twins," and it is associated with the twins Castor and Pollux in Greek mythology. In Egyptian astrology, the constellation was identified with twin goats, while Arabian astrology said it was twin peacocks.

For Parents: Gemini was also the namesake of the Gemini program, a NASA space mission in the 1960s that launched pairs of astronauts into space in the Gemini spacecraft. This constellation also inspired the names of the Gemini Observatory (twin 8.1-meter optical/infrared telescopes in Hawaii and Chile).

LEO: The constellation "Leo" is named after a mythical lion who was hunted by the legendary Greek hero Hercules. "Leo" is the Latin word for "lion."

LIBRA: This constellation's name means "the weighing scales" in Latin and is usually depicted as the scales held by the Greek goddess of justice, Astria.

For Parents: Libra was once considered a part of the Scorpius constellation. As a reminder of this, the brightest star in Libra, Beta Librae, has the name Zubeneschamali, which means "the northern claw" in Arabic, while Alpha Librae, Zubenelgenubi, is "the southern claw." Libra is the only zodiac constellation that represents an object, not an animal or a character from mythology.

ORION: Orion is one of the most recognizable constellations in the night sky. It is named after Orion, a hunter in Greek mythology.

For Parents: One of the stars that make up Orion is Betelgeuse, which is a red giant and one of the largest stars known. It is also the only star in the sky large enough and close enough to have been imaged as a disk in the Hubble Space Telescope. You might be able to see the difference in color between Betelgeuse and all the other stars in Orion (the star makes up Orion's right shoulder).

PEGASUS: Pegasus is named after a winged horse in Greek mythology that was sent by Zeus to fetch thunder and lightning from Mount Olympus.

PISCES: Pisces means "the fish" in Latin. It's really hard to see in the sky with the naked eye. Pisces is represented as two fish, attached by a cord.